Sylvia

Joyce Garvey

Best Wishes
Joyce Garvey

Joyce Garvey

Acknowledgements

To my family, my partner, and my friends for their love and support. To Bren, to the Bayside group, and to my agent, for their help and advice, and of course to the inspirational, Sylvia.

Book cover from a painting by Joyce Garvey.

Author's Photograph by Laelia Milleri.

Author's outfit by Claire Garvey.

DEDICATION

To James with love.

Joyce Garvey

THE BEGINNING

My page is white. A beam of morning sun filters in from the right hand side and colours it gold.

SYLVIA : THE GIRL WHO TALKED TO THE MOON.

CHAPTER I

PRISM

I blink: my eyes are open.

Above me is a pitched black sky: blank, no stars. I lift my hand up to my mouth. My breath is warm and damp: my fingers touch my eyes, my lips, my face. Still: I am.

Cautious as a clam I sit up. My sounds escape in question: marks. I see I am surrounded by some vast rock and through the depth of dark I hear the hollow wash of a sea sucking obsessively. My blue nightshirt is on as it was before. My feet are bare as they were before. The gold marital band on my finger is as before. I am.

'I pick the worms off me like sticky pearls.'

And I am standing up, wobbling and stumbling like some new born and bloodied fawn. My hand is over my mouth. My body feels and smells washed-out: as if it has been scrubbed, or rung out, or bleached, or all of these. My teeth are chattering but not with cold. My mouth opens: more consonants than vowels.

"Anybody there?" I call out to the moon, which hangs white as a knuckle in the black sky.

"Help?"

"Somebody?"

Clutching my sound close lest it trails away, I stand up now, wobbling and stumbling like some new-born and bloodied fawn. I wait for something: *anything?* Why is there is no vector here, no welcome? No cold hand takes hold of me and shakes. My mouth opens: more consonants than vowels:

"Hello? Hello? Hell-o-o-o?"

Pulling myself around, I turn my head quickly to catch some shadow but there is nothing there.. I can taste the tin of this dark night sky. I cup my hands and shade my eyes.

And then I see her. *Her:* my shadow self.

She is calling out at me. She is running, *her* blue nightshirt is shredded and torn, *he*r bare feet are kicking up the stones.

"Syl-l-v-i-a-aa-a!" She calls her name or mine?

I watch her run away into the night, the wind, the air. Her cry lingers long after she is gone.

"Syll-v-i-a-a-a-a a." I am inhabited by her cry. It flaps out, looking with its hooks for something to clutch.

'Sy-l-v-i-a-a-a-a a."

And I feel the cradle of my life rocking in some hallowed grave as I try to remember. I try to pull the shred of some life force back…

… till my last memories storm over me like spikes on a closing gate.

CHAPTER 2

FEBUARY 11TH 1963

MEMORIES AND THE BLUE/GREY MOTH

My last memory comes unblurred by emotion.

It is crisp and polished clear as glass *'sliding shut on some quick thing'* .
It was night there too, and I was in the kitchen of my house in Primrose
Hill. I was washing dishes. I held my plates to dip and wash and dip and
rinse and dry.

My plan was set and with this final deed I would *not* destroy myself but
put myself together. I held my plates to dip and wash and dip and rinse
and dry. Through verses I had dissected and ate life up. Now it was time
to tackle death. I held my plates to dip and wash and dip and rinse and
dry.

I had unlocked that which had built up inside me and systematically explored through my poetry the nexus of: (I remember I wrote down: eight words with bullet points):

- happiness
- anger,
- failure
- love
- lies
- nightmares
- revelations
- endings

I held my plates to dip and wash and dip and rinse and dry.

There were three of everything for my children and me. Three side plates, I dip, three bowls, I rinse, three cups, I dry: and how I took pride in the uneven number. He had been cut from my shelves. And cut from the house which I had cleaned from front to back and inside out. While the clock on the wall ticked out my plan.

Each dry dish was placed upon its shelf. My bare feet felt the wooden planks of the floor. I could smell the dead trees from which they came.

'*O golden child the world will kill and* eat.'

....

The towels and cloths were now piled up in my arms.

They were sweet smelling and clean and rightly so. They served me well.

"One, two, three, four, five…"

Would there be enough to seal the doors? Were they *too* big? But I was beyond myself so I already knew all the answers and all the solutions. My head was like a moon of pure acetylene. It floated so high.

I scanned the room upstairs. All must be ordered and correct: food placed where the sleeping children could stretch to reach, the window, wide to the air: the curtains drawn open. As I pulled them apart I felt their weft and weave close together in my hands.

And then... a blue/grey moth…

It flew in the wide open window and swooped, and flapped, and hovered all around the room. It settled on the wall.

So beautiful...

I squashed it dead and cleaned its blood spot off and, downstairs now, I tossed its last remains into the bin. Clink, clunk. My face pleaded with me from the shiny surface of the lid for one brief moment: clink, clunk.

Clink...and I was on my knees and the doors were sealed with tape and cloths and towels tight. And soon the smell of gas hissed over me like the ever-waiting snake.

The soft wind in my ears was my cold breath until the woman lay: her hands turned up.

CHAPTER 3

MOVING SHADOWS

There is nothing after that, but here.

I make a fist, then open it and study my palm.

These are *my* hands, *my* skin, *my* bones. I touch myself, my nose, my eyes, my mouth, my teeth. My mind is filled with *my* thoughts, Yes, I am Sylvia.

"Why am I here, moon?"

My last memories lie at my feet and rattle the rocks on which I stand. The moon is mute. He is nothing but a pock-faced orb who lights up my sins and judges me so. I smooth my night dress down. The sea is dragging behind it a dark crime.

"The dark crime is mine. Yes, I claim it, moon."

And now he knows my crime, I can see how he analyses me. Turning now in a circle I address the moon.

"Well?"

He turns his back on me and points a silver finger of light.

"Slylvia-aa-aaa."

It's her again, running and stumbling over rocks. I yell at her.

"Are *you* the prism of my fate or am *I yours?*"

The water stirs. I turn quickly to follow her, but *she* is as hidden now as *I* am on show. The land curves my face. I am a plot in the ground. I can hear crustaceans grow. The air is at home on me.

Yes, there is air.

I use it now to call again.

....

The moon answers.

He points his light behind me now and illuminates a wall of white, wet, stone. He colours it silver. It is a lighthouse:

The Lighthouse.

There is a force working. The Lighthouse hovers above me solid, filling me with its stare. Its light shines through my walls. My words seem said before.

"There were many, moon, who tried to put my *own* light out, for they were blinded by it. Do you *hear* that moon?"

The moon infuriates, pretending he is deaf. His face is drained dry and white as a knuckle. He shines right inside my eye. I do not flinch.

"See how I am *not at all* blinded by *you* moon or *your* lighthouse? It is powerless to illuminate what's closest to it."

The Lighthouse (I will call it that for I will make it mine) stands before me silent. And so I walk its circled path. It seems familiar to me or perhaps it is a theorem of some set trap? My hand is on the wall and I am climbing each step in the round, moving in a circle. I walk in a hollow '*groove of old faults deep and bitter.*'

Reaching the light I stop, listening for any sound. But there is no prize for reaching the top, no Pulitzer, no shining trophy waits in outstretched silken hand. Nothing moves. I am at sea. I am adrift surrounded by the cold scar of water. The moon watches from the sky. I am not yet his. I look him in the eye.

"Think again moon. The Lighthouse pleases me." I say. This will put him off his guard.

I lean on The Lighthouse walls, numb as a fossil. It tells me I'm here. It is *my* lighthouse and *I* am in control of its light.

I blink my eyes closed, and the light goes off.

Joyce Garvey

I blink my eyes open, and the light goes on again. I have decided. This is hell and hell exists? I note that it is a question. Death followed by eternity, must be the worst of both worlds, my poet once said. No night is safe from new of him.

And I write down THE LIGHTHOUSE in capitals, for I recognise its face.

Virginia Woolf wrote about a lighthouse once but *she* never got there. *This* light is all mine. I wallow in its beam.

But it takes light to cause a shadow. I turn my back and my other self is whispering in my ear, that this is but a lost light. She mutters to remember that *I* am *not* so great and that Virginia Woolf's books made mine possible. I find my shadow selfs whispering games so trite, so tiresome.

So, as she runs off, I shout at her another book: The Tibetan Book of the Dead. I tell her that I remember that period between death and rebirth.

"If this is it" I shout, "it will be *my* consciousness and not *yours* proceeding to enlightenment."

For she is nothing but the ghost of an infamous suicide.

The moon is dim and not one bit enlightened so I walk towards the sea. I am the master of my soul. She fears water but I feel its call. I wade in deep and bow my head and mouth open as wide as I can, I swallow its salt and sink.

The wet dark is above me. I wallow and surrender to its folds.

CHAPTER 4

TALK OF THE OTHER SELF

I blink, the light goes on and I am back on the rocks.

Death followed by eternity is the worst of both worlds.

I sit down on a rock and chip away its surface with my nails. I feel its pain as I scratch, and it feels mine. These rocks tell me how they once were soft and sand. They have hardened like my heart: the broken stones a saxifrage.

I curse, for she is back. She is whining and wringing her spindly hands. She is all over thin: arms waving like skinny windscreen wipers swinging back and forward as she runs and runs and runs. The sight of her pulls me like the proverbial sand, it slides and sucks me down. So now I scream, and scream, and scream and scream.

'There are tight wires between us. Pegs too deep to uproot.'

I close my eyes. I hold them shut tight as an old seashell. I do not hear what she shouts back before her voice fades into a sigh.

. . . .

Into the distance she runs, and hisses like the snake, she is. The moon's silver light weaves a parting in her hair and she is gone again.

"Moon did you see that great cave of loneliness reflected in the circles of her eyes?"

He turns away. Look how the moon denies it all.

'Bastard : Masturbating a glitter.'

But wait, he is sending in a sound, a shallow echo, like signals bats transmit to navigate the dark. The moon has brought a wave which rolls high and crashes hard against the rocks and in a whirlwind, ruptures and heals.

And then it stands erect, presenting me with something which makes me drop the shell...

...and hide.

Joyce Garvey

CHAPTER 5

WAVE 1939

• HAPPINESS

I am peering from behind The Lighthouse wall.

I see what has come in with the wave, it shapes into my space: an image radiant and solid as the day that is no more. Clear inside the wave I see, like on a great wide watery cinematic screen, that inside its curves there is a bright and beautiful day, coloured with glistening sun.

And there is a girl.

She is dancing. She skips in some field of corn or barley or wheat perhaps. A sea-bird flies, a spot of pink and gold beneath its wing. And she is holding up a shell. I lean forward, careful of my step. See, there's a boy: younger, running towards the girl, calling out to her. She turns her dance towards him now. Her soft hair flies in all directions as she pirouettes. Her dress is pink and scattered with flowers: primroses.

"Primroses moon, they are primroses, pink and white primroses, seventeen of them. I know this, for I have counted them. The girl is me, the dress is mine...It's *me*, moon!"

Crouching forward for a closer look, I see the girl fall down laughing in the corn. The breeze catches the edge of her dress and I can smell the grass. How sweet it smells. How wonderful.

And I am inside the wave as her. I feel the heat of the sun on my upturned face. Some bright force flies through my whole being down through the grass and into the earth. It is warm and bright and beautiful. There are more birds now, high in the clouds swooping and screeching.

My feelings are as high as those birds. Up in the air they soar, bumping into things, and swooping down on a stone building cracked with green, and a field of leaves trembling so like tongues. And there's my brother Warren, running, so alive, arms a rudder to the sky, making aeroplane noises.

"Look Sylvia I'm flying."

"Can't catch *me,* Warren?"

Blood thuds into my ears as I jump up and run towards him, then away and towards him once again, dizzy with the feelings of the sun, the flowers and the sweet scent of the day. I twirl and twirl. Shell to my ear, I am so gold like the centre of the daisy and I am so so happy. I glow like the light.

And then the knee of the wave turns down and it is over and I am back, left empty and dry as the rock I stand on.

The month of flowering's finished.

The fruits in,

Eaten or rotten. I am all mouth.

I am walking around and around and around now on ground level, circling The Lighthouse walls, muttering, with the other one hanging behind me.

'The woman is dragging her shadow in a circle.'

There is no sign of the wave now, but the sea is black and still. A mouth hole crying for location. The moon is dumb. I sit. I need to discipline my thoughts. I need to try to make some sense of this. That was me and my brother Warren, inside that wave. The house was ours in Winthrop, Massachusetts.

What year? I must think.

I must have been about seven and Warren, four. I remember now. My mother came (her feet were clad in yellow shoes, her skirt rolled up) and she brought us to the creek. There was a picnic in a wicker basket. I remember squashes and pumpkins, beheaded cabbages with wormy purple leaves and Warren and I had apple cake with lemonade which stood in tall glasses at a white, nervous-legged table.

And I remember the red, rust rocks, blue flowers cobalt as the sky, and the touch and smell of beech. I lay outstretched. That was the first time. The first time I realised completely what was meant by 'happiness.'

I pause and sift some pebbles through my fingers now.

My shadow self stands behind me and I can feel that she has grown stronger. She has stopped running and is halted high upon my rock.

My own blue nightshirt now has a tear.

CHAPTER 6

WAVE 1942:

• ANGER

How many times now have I climbed these lighthouse stairs?

I should have kept note, written Roman numerals on the wall and crossed them off each day like the prisoner I am. But there is no day. The time here is governed only by the lack of it. This sameness of it all though is beginning to *be* something to me.

'This is not death, it is something safer.'

I am looking through The Lighthouse window at the sea. It mirrors my face. Is it her or me? How long ago was it that we were one? And then I hear the silent echo come, which heralds in the memories.

Here is the wave, and all defences cast aside, I raise my sorry head to see inside its folds.

I am shutting my mouth on it: Communion: Body of Christ.

The new image in the wave is through a mirror with a younger me inside its glass.

I am a girl again with a girl face. I feel thin as a sheet, and crushed like there is a paperweight holding me down. I am in my school uniform adjusting a straw hat on my head and on the deep unquiet in my mind. My eyes are blank unwritten sheets. I try to straighten my school tie.

"What is the point of *things*?" I ask my reflection in the glass.

My collar is not clean, my blazer is creased. Does it matter if my hat is not straight or that my black shoe, in which I had lived like a foot, is scuffed?

The selfhood of things:

My father was dead.

This was his funeral day.

The hollow door opened for the darkness then. It took its chance. It made me angry. It reminded me that father told me many many times he would not die. He *promised,* but he lied. Even in his bones, he lied. I was betrayed.

"Must I see this day with his lies still stinging on my tongue?"

The moon does not reply but allows a black crowd of mourners in the wave to swamp my words. And there again is my brother, Warren, surrounded by nodding heads in long net veils. He is wailing his father's loss out to the sky as we procession file behind a carriage decked with scented white.

We move slow motion far along the road and way across the narrow bridge.

'Death-gowns,'

'Then two little feet.

The darkness surrounded me then and closed me tight. I was stone-faced and resolute. My hair was pulled back from my face so that all could see that my eyes were dry, and full of hate. I wanted to spit my anger out onto the wood holding my father in and watch it slide slowly over the brass of his coffin.

I was as cold as he.

And mother reached for me. Her hands were outstretched, her breath distilled, as my father was lowered, rope held. The brown earth shuddered his return. I would not take her hand, or the white rose to lay it on his head. I wanted to kick and kick and *kick* my father till he woke. I heard the sound of earth hit his coffin wood. It thudded into my ears. It ravished such waste.

I remember, too, the look on people's faces; a look for me, a terrifyingly sympathetic look. (There is no compensation for the death of a parent, no matter how many people move to guard and reach out to you. Their looks are wasted space.)

I was my own judge then.

And the wave turns in on me and on my anger and I am back at The Lighthouse once again with the wave trailing away with it my watery past. The anger of back then raises up again inside me now.

"You lied and left me father. You are to blame, Otto Plath? Why are you not here at The Lighthouse to help your daughter now? Again, my beloved father, you have left me in my need."

Abandoned child still, I am betrayed and whatever I do, I can't get back, back, back at him. Revenge dangles and taunts way out of reach, smouldering and burning me so with rage. It shakes my unforgiving heart and makes it pound. And she, my other self, is further away now but she shouts from the top of her rock. She is me and knows how to hit me hard like my flung rocks:

"Your *own* children?" Her raw words trail at me and seep into my bones.

I shut my eyes and all around drops in on me.

My other self is nearer to me now and I am climbing The Lighthouse stairs eyes shut, blind. A force races my steps and steams over me like the sea, and at each turn and blink, my children's faces haunt: tiny, bewildered, diminished.

New large tears appear in my nightshirt now.

I run and climb faster and faster and faster.

And at the third flight I fall.

When at last I open my eyes again I find that the moon has relented and waned. He shows me now a bell, in a hidden alcove on The Lighthouse wall. It hangs from a noose of rope that will not swing.

I raise my head and study its shape, and its shadow spreads against the wall. The bell's curves are green with living rust. Hard ridges and phosphorus circles groove its surface like a tree telling its age. But it is mute like the moon, encrusted, its symbols gathering old, left potency and stuck in time.

My fingers feel its hard core and I remember another bell.

Where are these memories flung from?

Like a beam of light they are delivered and lain at my feet. A past but not forgotten bell is ringing out. It is the bell that my father rigged to call us to the fields where he kept his hives of bees.

My father revered his bees.

"Father", I hurl my heart. The bees are flying. They taste the Spring. "Father".

And I am a girl again and I am at his knee and he is telling me how Darwin enkindled his interest in biology and bees. He told me how bees flapped their wings so fast that they created vortices like small hurricanes and I would run around the room flapping my arms up and down: trying to out fly the bees.

Deep inside my heart, I knew that I never could compete with his bees and deep down my father scared me with his neat moustache and his Luftwaffe ways. I knew how his body opened and shut, but his mind, was always closed to me. *His* laughter though was warm but much too seldom. I hear it now for *he* sees, as *I* do, the irony here.

My father still has a hold of me.

And just as I feel his breath mingle with mine, the wave washes the image away into the core of its labyrinth. And so I turn on the moon.

"Where is my father now ? Where is Darwin? Are they colluding with you in this cardboard space, with me as the experiment?"

"Father, are you working on a follow up to your book 'Bumblebees and their ways'? Will you call it 'My daughter and her Ways?' Will I be tagged and studied and categorized as some rare species of treacherous woman?"

This paralyses the running Sylvia. She stumbles and falls. I turn my back on her and the moon and shout my wrath out at my father once more.

'You died before I had time-

Marble-heavy, a bag full of God-'

You died.'

But he'd sooner return to his queen bee than to his princess:

The bees found him out

Moulding onto his lips like lies

And in this crack of time I wish I'd found him out. I wish that I had mourned for him the way I should and then perhaps 'the unfinished' would not have haunted me so, and made me ill.

The tethered thing inside my head would never fly for it was half-formed and broken, without wings and without hope.

CHAPTER 7

WAVE 1953:

• FAILURE

My eyes are open and I am studying the bell.

In the hidden alcove it lies with a noose of rope that will not swing. I raise my head and study its shape and its shadow spreads against the wall. Before the moon knows it, I am working to clean and free the bell. I am so committed. I am taking pride in it.

Pride mixed in with self-love: all are rooted in the same inarticulate centre of me. I love to feed myself on my food of pride.

"Kiss me, moon, and you will see how important I am?"

I am scraping away the rust from the bell rope with a sharpened shell. I will bring this back to life. I am dwelling on the complete and utter importance to me, of being recognised as having achieved.

This yearning boiling inside of me: was it inherited?

The powdered rust rises and filters through the air and mingles with my breath until I have cleaned the rope which holds the bell and I have worked it free. My shadow self is back and screaming

"Free! free! free?"

The moon is on her side. But I would and will do what I did all over again to spite them both. The rope is strong and dry in this world preoccupied with water. I am forming the rope into a noose.

The moon is blanketed in bees. Z z z z z…

The beam which holds the rope is also strong. It swings above the flight of stairs.

And I remember a rope which once I formed to pretend I would strangle my mother. I practiced on the air.

"Mother, mother, I will choke the life from you!"

I throw the moon a glance. His cratered dome is down as I pile up the stones:

one,

two,

three,

four.

One more slab of stone and I can reach the hanging noose.

My shadow self has called out to the moon. The moon wakes suddenly, sour, sweet honeyed onion now. He makes a move and sends the signal to the wave. I lull him into thinking what I *make* him think.

And I add to this, by quoting Joyce at him.

"Hold onto the now, the here, through which all future plunges to the past. ..'

He is clouded now for he is confused trying to work out the quote (just as Joyce himself intended so.) Reaching out to touch the bell's surface cast in time, I hear the coming of the wave.

This time I will not run to see what picture of me the wave brings in. Watching from the window now I hear the rush of water against the stones. They beat my past to death. I will not move. And so the image comes reflected on The Lighthouse wall of glass, glistening in wet.

The rope to strangle swings beyond my reach. For here is the image, and the image is the devil woman herself. Here she is.

Aurelia. My mother stares me in my third and evil eye.

She is silhouetted on the wall now like some wide technicolour screen. Even here in this hell, I can't escape her. My shadow self sees her opportunity and states that without my mother I wouldn't exist. I answer her:

"Our mother and our father between them have split us into two."

"Therefore, moon, I do not have to take this mother witch now. She intends me to wilt in this concocted heat. I will not." For I am all grown up. I spit at her. Look how *grateful* this dead crone is? I hurl a stone into my mother's face. The glass cracks.

From her:

'I have suffered the atrocity of sunsets.

Scorched to the root.

Aurelia face refuses to bruise. But wait...there beside her in the wave, there am I. The wilted rose that bloomed out of her. The wave has my attention now.

I am lying in some hospital bed with my hands and my tongue tied. I am broken.

I am away; strange. The dark bird, the thing which slept in me, is awake. Its sly feathery turnings, its malignity, is scraping and pecking inside my head. I feel its thoughts and feel them now.

'Is there no way out of this mind?'

See how I was? How I lay lamenting the world around me? The white room clutched me in its grasp. I smell that space. I hear the metal noise of wheels and feel them place inside my mouth a block of wood, bitten before by many teeth. White men crowded me in.

While my mother sat and watched them torture me. She sat fingering her beads. The serpent of rejection had hissed failure in my ear. Harvard has turned me down and kicked a hole inside my head. My writing 'did not meet their standard'. Just like I never met *her*s: my mother fingers her beads.

"They were your pills?" I shout at her now or then?

I took all *her* pills (see how *she* tried to kill me?) and I crawled under the wood beams and waited for the dark to come and take me in its arms.But the sun burnt through the grey blue layers of fog and dragged me out: bleached.

I had tried to confront immortality itself and failed. It was my mother, that bead mover, who made me fail. And then she brought me to be 'cured.'

*'Heating the pincers, hoisting the delicate hammers, 'A current agitates the wires Volt upon volt...' I 'sizzled in the blue volts '.*And see how my mother fingered and fingered the beads around her neck while *my* head rolled.

"Are you alright Sylvia?"

If I had succeeded in becoming a Harvard scholar she would *have had* to be proud of me which was something alien to her.

Perfection is terrible. It should never have children.

CHAPTER 8

WAVE:1956

• LOVE

The sea pitches and rolls in the waves

There are a cemetery of memoirs drifting by. These times in my life come at me trailing blood and sinews and familiar things long gone: a crimson hat, a flickered candle in some breeze, a touch of hand, a smell of grass and weed and mottled cork.

"What is your point moon?"

And I pick up a stone and hurl it at his face. It does not reach its mark by a thousand million miles or so, but turns on a tangent. Down and down it falls and catches the running Sylvia in her stride. She falters, stumbles, but runs on.

Where does she think she is going?

....

I am writing my epitaph on the white wall of The Lighthouse where the moon can see.

Sylvia. Poet. *Daddy and mummy, I'm finally through.'*

I who have filled my life with words can think of nothing to say.

I am still all over hate. It holds me together, this 'getting back' at them.

"Do with me what you will moon." He has bleached me with its light.

The moon, who is my sentence, is only fit to show me pictures.

....

My hair, is bleached as he, and shines blonde from inside the dark folds of the new wave which floods my memories now. I look to see for there is nothing left to do.

A mottled mirror of my past, I see me there, a fully-fledged woman. I am twenty-three or twenty-four perhaps and blond. The White Goddess, I thought myself. Was that the year…? I peer to see. Its nineteen fifty-six. I know this year so well.

Look and learn moon.

The image is a crowded room. It comes with such noise and force. The music: Joe Lyde Jazz; the lights and chatter like the zoo. It's a party full of life and colour and swing: white noise of the elegy with that blare all over it. This party is the ONE. It is in Cambridge, England. I am a Fulbright scholar: the American, and how I flaunt it! '

The outsider holds court holding herself carefully'.

There I am, inside the wave. A woman in red, head back and laughing.

The little crowd around me clings like whelks to rocks and laughs along with me. But the wet wit on my tongue is not for them. My loud merriment is centred in one direction only. My laugh is too forced. I try too hard for attention from across the room. His tall figure stands: his back is to me.

At last he turns.

And here at sea I have to turn as well. This is too sore. My nails dig into my arm but here the only pain I feel is deep inside my head.

But the draw of the wave is too strong and so I turn back and I am me inside the wave and the hurt is the pain of lust and it is excruciatingly wonderful. The object of my desire watches now. I want to run to him and fall at his feet. I watch me and weep.

My head is crowned with thorns. My bones are numbered. Look at me? I am there and I am laughing. That laugh (for the judges, the strangers, the frighteners), has pulled him to me. He turns from his close-knit group and let's his eyes feel every part of me in one slow glance.

"Oh great and mighty God and all the Demons too: the feeling, moon!"

I have no control. My mind flies off and leaves my body limp and rigid all in one. His eyes are dark with sin, his shock of hair holds earth, and wind and fire, and he turns again to take another look: his Neptune opposite my Ascendant exactly fixed.

And I am away mad, girl inside a nightmare of longing.

'-All wants, desire

Falling from me like rings'

"This feeling inside me moon? I'd forgotten the intensity of it: the pull of the rope of desire: the sheer giddy excitement stirring my heart." With my slender sling poised towards my Goliath, I had changed into the Goddess of War. The battle was on.

Look how I charge? I am so stupid with confidence.

Look how my sword too is drawn and I am holding court with false cheerful brilliance quoting lines from Yeats. The noise and laughter in the room bubbling over in my eyes while all the time I am aware.

'There is a panther stalks me down.'

But see how I fear him not? I'm walking towards him now, cigarette outstretched begging for a light. I look like some painted clockwork toy.

My steps are slow and measured. My eyes focused on my goal. This was the first time that I met my poet, and Chaucer would have feared and shook his sorrowful head as the scorpion wove towards the panther, baring her claws.

'The only thing to love is Fear itself.'

The room seemed to turn and watch as he lit up my cigarette. I saw the Dante fire inside his eyes.

'I have a fire for you in my mouth: Scorching relentlessly '

But *he* was the fire and *I* was ice. He melted me.

And yes, of course I saw the danger in it all: the loaded crossbow. I feel it now as I watch. My ant soul prostrate under his glance, my red flag waving at the Gods. And I was wearing the shoes, the red ones, but he said blue to suit his rhyme? He was wrong. I was no cobalt jewel.

He saw that too and swept me to a panelled room and kissed me red and hard, and with one whiff of that beast, it gave me hope, and when I bit him on the neck to taste his blood, the bad cat's claim (See how I tried too hard,) he licked his blood from off my tongue.

Cannibal: how did you taste?

And then he left with someone else.

The wave falls back and leaves me still and shuddering. I feel the other Sylvia at my back. I do not turn but feel her anguish, as my memory dwells on love and lust. That first night that I met my poet, huge derrick-striding Ted with poems and richness, I was instantly in love. Chaucer would have sighed. And I, wrote in my journal:

'Consider yourself lucky to have been stabbed by him;

... rip-and glory in the temporary sun of his ruthless force-'

Can you see how I was poisoned by him right from the very start. As he of me. We tore into each other and slotted perfectly in. We were 'a planetary certainty according to Prospero's Book' he said. My worship needed a God and I had found him. And the feeling in me then, was plain raw want.

'In the month of red leaves I climb to a bed of fire.'

"Oh how I remember and miss so that flaming of life that resolute fury of existence." But even through it all he put me down.

He edited in his 'oh so cool' review that the poem I sent for print was fraud.

"Fraud, do you hear that, moon?"

I picture him now, head down, shocked black hair, fallen shadow across his face, under the bell glass of the wave, some handsome fish he was. 'This poem tells me Fraud' he wrote and with a stroke of his pen he took control. And the more he put me down the more I yearned to be possessed by him, and soon I was. And we created an Eden in which the fallen me mingled with my show self's crystal tears while yellow demons sprouted from the lips of my jaundiced Adam.

The moon's horns plunge and toss.

For now the wave has my poet and me lying still in our bed. There is a handmade patchwork quilt. My panther's arms are wrapped around me warm as a winter cloak and he is deep in sleep. I feel the heat. I owned him then, my panther tamed.

But wrong again... The beast belonged only to himself. The lair was his.

It is *his* tiny flat I see, looking even smaller now? I'd forgotten that faded quilt thrown over the bed till now. I made that quilt. It's the one I worked on after each of my rejections: Listen and take note? Rejected poems sent back from gob-stopped mouths: they made that quilt. Rejections: clean on the printed page, turned down. I see them woven deep inside the warp and weft.

The wave is showing me round the tiny bedroom we loved in then. The moon is some B film maker. And the room obliges in technicolour: it is beautifully untidy. Such Victorian squalor and how we wallowed in the mess of soft porn, and loud rows, with shaking walls, seals barking from the nearby zoo, and bees humming words of my father's long forgotten songs.

Always it seemed summer, even in the Spring, with pansies and primroses, and my panther ate them all. It was a labyrinth he said, a Knossos of coincidence all enclosed in one bedroom, nowhere to hide, at a whole six guineas a week.

I watch me there as I write my poems backed against that bulging wooden cupboard of our things. The storerooms were full of hearts. It was glorious. It was marvellous. I feel now how much we loved? We were one, poets together, he in one corner working, me in the other, apart, yet matched together, a rhyming-couplet, a sonnet, a haiku of seven wonders.

And I am up and writing at my desk inside the wave. I can smell the walnut (mixed with polish from a tin) from that old wood desk? The house was possessed he said. He told me that I haunted it.

But wait, the wave has moved me on. And now I see a street in early morning.

How incredible it is. Stunningly beautiful, full of bird song, mottled with morning sun and long limbed trees laden with leaves staring at the clouds. And mayflies, silver; whirring light and orbiting the sun. Tequila and salt on the tongue: burn on the hand: cymbals clanging with sound: filling my head to burst open in yellow and indigo and purple and blue.

And then in a blink I'm walking along a familiar road. The crisp burst of leaves rush and sift through the antenna of time under my step. My sandals are yellow like the sun, and there is another letter in my hand to post to Aurelia.

"Mother, come to London, Ted and I are getting married." I came right to the point of it.

I raise my head to the sun inside the wave and feel its rays penetrate my skin for I was fixed in bliss in glorious anaesthetic. In only four months since our eyes first met my handsome poet and I would be one. And I would be at last fulfilled:

'Gratified

All the fall of water an eye

Over whose pool I tenderly

Lean and see me.'

The other Sylvia rises up to turn the wave. It moves away to her bid.

Her stones are piled higher now than mine. In less than four months, yes, my poet and I were married.

On June 16th (Bloomsday chosen specially for our mentor James Joyce) in the Church of St George the Martyr, Queen Square, London, Ted and I were joined together in marriage. I write it onto the rock.

My mother answered my plea and came to London to witness the event. And event it was. We had four seasons in one day. The buds opened in my posy of Magnolias. The rain drenched Aurelia's hat and turned it from purple to blue. The sun set orange and then the wind blew frost against our skin.

It was perfect. *We* were perfect. We had a new and spacious home. We were a couplet versed in stars, a sonnet of seasons, yes, yes, a haiku of seven wonders.

"Living with Ted, moon, was like being told a perpetual story. His mind was the biggest, most imaginative I had ever come across."

Never in my life had conditions been so perfect: a magnificent handsome husband, a quiet, large house with no interruptions, phone, or visitors; the sea at the bottom of the road, the hills at the top. Mental and physical well-being ensued. Each day I felt stronger, wider awake. And I could feel a new direct pouring of energy into my own work. I was gathered tight with golden light, with his hand held securing mine.

And life begun minutely to take care of itself.

....

And the wave turns its watery leaf and shows ..

...my poet and I walking hands joined together, through shadowed paths and sunlit fields. We are talking and talking and talking. We are deeper, and sombre and opening up inside a myriad of new subjects and titles. This was the green grass of wonderful Yorkshire now. The countryside was ours and vast and quiet, bar our love and laughter. We roamed the fields and ponds in search of hawk and owl and pike, never letting each other go.

The moor had noises of its own: we said it was haunted by Cathy and Heathcliff.

I climbed trees doing what, he said, Emily Bronte could never do. And the moor-wind came as I recited poems to her. My poet said he wondered what Emily would have made of my suggestive tone, of my frisky glances and my liberties and the hot stink of his fox!

There was tapping on our window panes for we were beginning to fulfil our dream.

Ted's book 'Hawk in the Rain' had won the New York poetry prize and he was to be published by Harper in the summer. The beginnings of success shone inside the glass dome. Ted would be the first to make his name and that would make it so much easier for me when *I* was accepted.

We shared our visions with extreme intensity. We were utterly loyal. He helped me fight my soul battles and stood guard against my demons while I encouraged his 'claws and cages' verse till he perfected it.

Nothing short of excellence would do.

I was the most vivid presence in his life as *he* was in mine. And my mind, too, was clear. I would write until my words spoke from my deep self. I would explode like Matisse and colour my words in success, and then I would have my children and speak even deeper.

I believed.

'everything is writable about if you have the outgoing guts to do it and the imagination to improvise.'

The wave turns and drags my written words away.

CHAPTER 9

WAVE : JUNE 1959

WAVE: APRIL 1960

• LIES

On the white of The Lighthouse wall I draw my face.

Using a charcoal stone the wave has tossed up, I give my body a fish's tail. Some black mermaid I am.

'Among fish and frogs the soul hides like a pupa.

'Drawing was something that always served to calm me. Did I draw till I had the scene prisoner so that *I* might have a chance to escape? I write *that* down inside my mind. The moon takes note. And now my watery postman of wave what delivery do you have for me this night? What tale of woe thrown from your slimy throat will you hurl at me now?

I am ready to analyse. (Note how I am both observer and observed.)

There I am. I am sitting on the grey settee in our flat in Primrose Hill in London. I have my sketch book on my knee and I am drawing me with a fish's tail. Open on the table in front of me is a letter. (See how my life was governed by the written word?) Heinemann want to publish The Colossus, (these were the forty poems I wrote before we left America).

So: this is the breakthrough that I have been praying for, this is my chance to shine as much as he, so why do I draw and not dance. See how even when I feel I have achieved I cannot rejoice. *It*, the tethered bird, moves inside me telling me that I will not follow through, but fail *after* the success. I *will* me to enjoy just once, but see it is a waste of the time I do not have.

"Dance, dance wherever you may be, I am the Queen of the dance says she" .

Inside the wave I only throw the letter down on the wooden table covered with his papers and his pens. And then I am up and I am locking the door behind my letter of success and walking out into the London day.

I'm watching me, sitting on a bench. Trafalgar Square: hot sun: red tops of great double decker busses moving to the right, black cabs, white highlights: sun high at the left, green leaves in granite oblong basins: traffic roar: flap and flight of pigeons round and round the base of Nelson's Column: round, and round, and round, circling people's feet and their own white-shit, and I am feeling sick.

I ask the pigeons where they go to die?

I rub my stomach. I am so, so, pregnant. The child inside me holds me together. See how it is stronger than me? Inside me lies a soul as from the hand of God. And *still* I can't rejoice. I am writing in my journal:

'Children might humanise me. But I must rely on them for nothing.

Fable of children changing existence and character as absurd as fable of marriage doing it.

Happiness is the first stage of sadness. Fact.

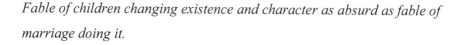

I am a weakling and a masochist. I say it quietly though so my shadow self does not hear. For presented to me now is another memory raw from the cauldron. Here is this sad, caged birdlike creature. Look how its eyes dart around in watchful anxiety.

Yes moon, It's me I see and so different from before. Where there is an idea of Paradise there is also the idea of the fall. For now my step is slow as snail: suctioned and slimed in living as in death.

It is England again. I have had my way. But it is not the rain bowed life that I had hoped for. In England my poet is surrounded by success and adoring students. How they hung on his every word. I am the walking living: walking in the London cold. Winter is in the air and in my heart. My head is hung. All that I thought I had is drifting away. My marriage bed is turning down. Each day the story is the same.

My poet leaves me home cooking dinner destined for the trash. The child inside me makes me sick and ugly fat. He turns away from such a sight.

I can only hear his voice.

It doesn't call my name.

But yes, I love him still. He is my capital, my God, myself, for all my sins. I wait and make a home.

I have hung our cave with roses

With soft rugs-

But I remember now the real reason though why this sadness and despair has ripped a hole inside my head inside the wave, inside my soul:

It is shame. I feel it now. I had committed a crime, an unforgivable crime, a green, a blue, a black, a purple crime. In a fit of jealous murderous rage I had ripped up all Ted's work in progress: his poetry and his plays and the book of Shakespeare that he loved much more than me. I tore them up, and they tore me.

Sometimes you have to do something bad to stop yourself doing something worse.

But 'I cannot ignore this murderous self. I smell it and feel it but still I will not give it my name.'

And she is on her run again. My shadow self, Sylvia running and running in the night wet. The moon shines a spotlight on her. She is some spindly bird. I turn from her.

"Moon where do all the dead birds go? No not here I know there are none. Back in the land of the living: where are all the dead bird bodies?"

The moon ignores me. He has no time for trivialities. He asks me instead about the letter I had in my hand.

Deluded words: try these.

"Well?"

The letter was to my mother telling her how happy I was in London, England. Yes I have said, I got my way. We were in England. There. Read the letter and be damned. My words were red:

"London is a delight. Ted is doing so well, published and on radio now. We've found a flat, 3 Chalcot Squar, invested in a marvellous bed, a stove and an American refrigerator .'

See how I gush out *things* at her to please her ever demanding finger of point. Mother, mother, I can never let you know the truth: no frown of mine will ever betray the company I keep.

"Are you *happy* now moon, happy that you have read my letter of deception, happy that you have caught me inside all my lies?"

I suck at you moon and my mother, from the Black Sunday streets of Camden Town, as the letter disappears through the mouth of the red lipped-box. Posted.

And I note that in London there are no dead bird bodies on the ground, on roofs of buildings or underneath the trees.

....

I am cleaning the bell again. It is its turn, for here there are so few items to devote my attention to. Strange, how I came from a world cluttered with things and now they can be counted on one hand. I'm wondering: that here in this now: if each thing chosen has a significance. The moon thinks that only *he* is my only significant other. I sit beside the bell on the stone step: two objects, both not functioning as was intended.

"By who?"

At least I have the power to rescue the bell. I look into its face. It has ceased in silent shame. Its chain is stuck and will not move. It's locked in time. I have the power to free the bell. What is going on under all this grit and grime which in itself lives? And now I am killing it.

And I remember the blue/grey moth...

I scrape: away. I scrape: away. I hear it die. As I work and work at the surface with a sharpened shell, a little patch of the real bell is born out of the destruction. It comes: death in life: its own spectre?

'The moon lays a hand on my forehead.'

....

And now I am lying face up to the night sky on my familiar rocks. The Lighthouse glistens and pales my right hand side with its light. There is something about a lighthouse. I always said I'd like to live in one.

But this was not living.

I ask the vast body of white looming above what it _is_ to me: guidance over rough water? Stability? Change? Virginia Woolf wrote about a lighthouse once, but she never got there. The other me runs past now shouting that Virginia Woolf's books made mine possible. I shout at her another book, The Tibetan Book of the Dead. I shout back at her that I remember that period between death and rebirth.

"If this is it," I shout, "it will be _my_ consciousness and not _yours_ proceeding to enlightenment,

She is nothing but the ghost of an infamous suicide. I blink; the light goes on. I blink the light goes off.

"Remember _I_ am the one in control." Why do I shiver at this thought?

"Looking back now moon would you say it was America or England? Which country brought me down?"

He refrains from answer and implies he doesn't like my 'turn of phrase'. Why blame my ills on a country. He is a pig.

"Grunt on pig". How is that for a turn of phrase?

And anyway, I have no time to argue with him over words when I am busy with my tasks. Can you see how my bell is coming up a treat. My sharpened shells are nearly worn down.

The whole right side of the bell is shining with half my face Picasso-esque in it. If I tilt it to the left I can see the moon. The moon looks away. He won't commit: another non-committer then? I answer my own question. "England and America *both* brought me down moon." I wanted so much from both of them.

'Perhaps when we find ourselves wanting everything, *it is because we are dangerously close to wanting nothing.'*

They were her words, my therapist.

I hear me telling her that old refrain: 'I *don't know who I am. I want I think to be omniscient...I think I would like to call myself "The girl who wanted to be God." Yet if I were not in this body, where would I be?...But, oh, I cry out against it. I am I-I am powerful, but to what extent? I am I.'*

....

Now I am sitting on the top stair of the lighthouse. I have cleaned the lense. The moon is pleased. His face turns and I note his difference.

"You are changing moon."

See how he has changed in this place made of past sins and tangled atoms where everything else remains the same: he has changed. Now he is a full and perfect circle and summons to the sea. But I'm not interested. Go away with your images. What's done is done. But everywhere I turn the image settles in front of me till I give in and shut my mouth on it.

....

I am surprised to see that the sun is shining in my eyes inside the wave again. I am baked like a cake. But I am not feeling its rays. Wait:

Am I expected to remember why?

This is the inside of our flat in London once again. I am looking out onto the leafy street. I turn a glow of contentment now. I am mistress of my own imagery in blissful numbness. Ted has forgiven me for my jealous fits and I have realised it's only me he idolises.

Ah how *touching.*

And look how content I have become and look how I cook and Ted too. He's feeding me orange juice, half a cold peach, and kisses and he's reading to me from 'The Sun also Rises'. We are sleepy candlelit warm and constructive...for once not mad cross-reference annihilation and destruction; wilfully and diabolic. We are calm and bourgeois.

I am feeling though that I must be idolised, for see how clever I am?

I am published many times now, I have finished my latest verse and inside of me grows my greatest accomplishment yet: the boy he always wanted grows inside and feeds my pride. The signs were right. I say it in good sentences.

I tidy my tarot cards from off the coffee table.

'*The air crackles with blue tongued lightening-haloed angels.*'

I stare into the wave and there is Ted wrapping his arms around me: head against me. I smell his just washed hair. I feel his breath on mine. I am in the special place. I belong and I deserve it so. He kisses the back of my neck then moves off to tidy things away in the wooden cupboard I have painted blue to match the sky.

I watch him walk through the arched door. I thought it gave the place a classical touch. Ted laughed and said:

"Keep dreaming moon-girl."

And there is that drawing I did of Boston lakes. It has been framed and sits above the dresser with the floral plates we bought in Spain. The lamp has a fringed scarf thrown over it to soften my mood. And my mood is playing music in my head. A love song for its love I feel. Ted is rubbing my stomach and feeling new life kick and happiness flies around the room and opens up in a rainbow over us.

My feelings are so high in the air of light and trust, and motherhood again (all pending) and knocking on our door is a young couple come to view our flat. I feel elated as I show them around

We shall need a bigger place, I tell them, In the country to raise our family, I tell them, to keep bees, I tell them, to grow flowers and vegetables and write, I tell them. And they listen well and I, I like the look of them.

I see the couple in the wave. The sea has lied to me. I insist Ted lets them have our flat. A wonderful couple, he is a writer and she is dark but *so, so* like *me* in thoughts and word. They are just right I say, we *must* let them have our flat. It's meant to be.

And they write down their names, for us to call:

David and Assia Weevil.

My self has turned her back on me.

Joyce Garvey

CHAPTER 10

WAVE: SEPTEMBER 1961

• NIGHTMARES

The moon is pissing me off.

His lack of response is irritating in the extreme. I kick out at the cardboard quality of this place. I can do nothing with this flat, flat, flatness and the lack of *colour and tone* that's here.

If this is hell, then I deserve to be punished better. I deserve more pain.

"Pay me *some* attention, moon" You are my therapist now.

"Listen?"

This space is so empty. The emptiness shapes into me.

There is no life in the sea. I could leave my mark here if only I could find some depth. Some fiddler crabs creeping in sideways fashion which once scared me to hell but now I would stretch out my hand for them to pinch. I want to feel pain now and not just in my thoughts.

What I would give for the sting of a bee.

And I remember again my father and his bees. and how he tended them. Yes, he loved them more than me. I imagined myself then as a bee: the queen:

'Is she dead? Is she sleeping?-

-With her lion-red body, her wings of glass?'

And then a thought? Is my father somewhere mourning for me?

If I'd have mourned for him could that have been the exorcism I needed to make me whole: to heal me? His ghost is inseparable from my pain. And the air fills with Eros whispering my father's name. as the wave rises up and takes my thoughts.

"Listen moon and I will tell you how my poet and I moved from the city to the country mess of Court Green Devon: our new home. The house had called us to it. A dream was coming true. But when dreams come true, nightmares are also realized.

"How I know that now, moon".

The force was hurling towards me.

'-The indefatigable hoof-taps.

Our new house was like a person responding to our love and attention.

'It has castle thick walls and ten rooms which wind around a cobbled courtyard. "I wrote." Ted has set himself up an office under the high pitched thatch of the attic and is out now digging up a big vegetable garden. There are laburnum, lilacs and roses." I wrote it out.

I felt the roses in my soul then. The air so fresh with flowers and trees.

This was how it was to be happy.

I had carved a tiny front lawn out of the wilderness and I filled nooks and crannies with flowers from the un-weeded garden, in pewter, china, and copper cooking pots.

I wrote with angels in my heart.

I intended keeping bees and we were growing vegetables and we would be self-sufficient: self…'I will find my true self ', I wrote…and added: 'Already we are eating some home-grown food. We are using a nice round dining table lent to us by David and Assia Weevil who have taken over our flat in Chalcot Square.'

The wave washes the sentence away trailing with it peach coloured gladiolus and the buzz of bees from our 'Garden of Eden'. And my shadow self is buzzing like a wayward bee and still runs and runs and runs. Does she never tire or think to slow down? And I am back cleaning the bell. I look up at the moon. He is still full but changing little by little.

"I want to tell you something about bees."

"Yes it is relevant. Do not disturb my train of thought. Bees...and my father."

I have the moon's attention now. And I feel the anxiety all beekeepers feel as they open their hives after a closed winter.

I move my shell brush in gentle strokes across the bell as I talk.

"Bees don't just pollinate flowers and give us honey." I look up at the moon. His attention is on me.

"Some bees are soldiers, some hunters and gatherers," the moon still watches." And some are undertakers born to bury the dead." My father cared so for his bees. They sang his eulogy *in 'furious Latin.'*

The moon looks down in funeral veil and I am at work to clean my bell. But I...

I am smug as a virgin:

In my white hive-

Seeing off my honey quietly humming.

I have the moon off guard. I have him round my finger making signs. I knew he would send me the wave so I could study the bees and here it is. I lay down my arms. I have a plan. I wish to note how bees work together to serve their queen.

And I observe me now, I am tending my own bees. I observe how this Queen bee who should be strong enough to kill off all her rivals: I see now how she controls and manages.

I call out to the moon. I crave my audience.

"Moon this is Devon again and our cottage in Court Green. Turn you heap of withered crust and look?"

See first how the cottage has grown with our love. There are flowers: lilac, I can smell their scent, and patches of root and green where vegetables reach up to the blue and tall trees and hedges trim and there I am.

"Moon look how the cottage has taken it all from me?"

I am drawn tight, and brown and tumbled like a lone and tangled weed, I'm throwing things around me and cursing like some crone-crow: tending the bees and wishing my father was there to point me out the workers and tell me why some move in one direction while others stay put. I am frayed.

And now I have numbly knocked aside their sugar feeder and I am stung all over.

"Tell me what to do father?" No answer.

Traitor: Abandoner. All creation is jammed in his selfish soul. He continues to let me down and down and down.

But wait...

The wave throws me a needle right through my eye.

....

Here is my child, Nicholas smiling and gurgling from his garden pram beside the toddling Freida. I have placed them in the shade of the elm. Nicholas: I rush to move him away from the furious bees dragging Freida with him.

I pull them deep under the wych elm. The elm shows me the wrongness of it all. The bees fly all around.

Why did I call this wave?

That elm haunted me, moon? Between the tap root of that tree it shows me nothing but my faults entwined and spread and wormed inside. It can see into my future.

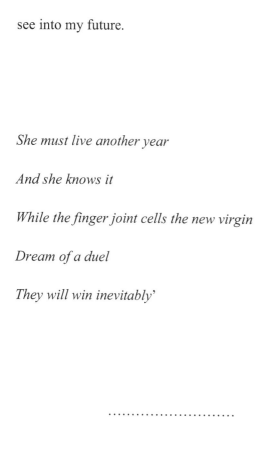

She must live another year

And she knows it

While the finger joint cells the new virgin

Dream of a duel

They will win inevitably'

....

The bees turned on me. This is not death but something worse. For in death I would not have to face the consequences of life. The moon lays a hand on my shoulder: black-faced and mum as a nurse. But see how, if I cannot be the queen, I have become the worker bee and I work and work to clean the bell to shine the windows and the lighthouse lens and sweep the stairs and work to block the thoughts I've called upon myself.

The other Sylvia is scratching at her eyes and face with pointed fingers of her hand. While mine move in circles scraping at the bell.

The bell shines back at me: the sharp shell I am using to scrape away the rust, it cuts my hand. She screams. I suck the pain.

And I remember the pain which descended like a thick and heavy cloak over my beloved Devon. I became my words then and there was no time in my day to write them down. My poet was so taken up in building his tower of fame and I became the house frau: so left behind: so lonely. I needed help. Someone to tell, someone to confide in, someone to curse at life with. So I packed my child up and set off to London to see my friend, Assia Weevil.

We could help each other. She was always telling me how city life wore her down. She needed a country break to free her mind and she did so love Freida and Nicolas.

None of her own she envied me my children.

Maybe we could do some deal. I needed someone to take care of them while I worked and she wanted some country air to fill her city lungs. Even one day in a fortnight perhaps?

And the wind blew and let it be so.

............…................…..

The bell sparkles now with my elbow grease, and I work, and work, and work and work.

"In summer, moon, bees only live for six weeks...

...They work themselves to death."

...........…..............

The moon has his back to me and as I clean The Lighthouse windows for the umpteenth time. I'm thinking about the meaning or lack of meaning of how it is we humans deal with living together.

And I am off on a tangent. I cannot make us out at all, no matter how I think I grew to understand a little better how we humans live, through my study of the bees. I learned just how the bees all pulled together to serve the Queen and how she gave her life to serve them in return.

Inside my country home I seemed directly linked with nature and possessed the power of generating new life. Just like *you* moon with your three phases of waxing, full, and waning. (And now I am a waning crone: or dead crone: fourth phase?)

I see my face as I shine the lens. It looks to be floating in the dark night sky. And I wonder who I am.

"Do we ever know moon?"

The moon turns on me and I am lost in the robes of all his light. He lifts the bell jar off and reminds me...That all that time in my cottage of country bliss, another bee had laid her sweet and sticky trap.

'A curtain of wax'...

The wave hurls more salt against the lens. It will never be clean.

And I give up and set off in chase of the running Sylvia.

And she is weeping loud and I am laughing at the pair of us running, running, running, inadequate breasts bouncing, spindly legs kicking up the stones.

....

I run in a circle. Circles always scared me. The music of a carousel always frightened me as a child. There is no end to circles here and no escape. The other Sylvia knows. That's why she is running round, and round and round. I hear the music in the wave now. It heralds something I fear so I am compelled to watch. I am telling Assia Weevil about the birth of my child she cradles in her arms.

The scream is mine, I say. I am hanging on to a white nurse. I make a point of it and laugh. The pain encompasses me. I do not want my poet near. I push him away. The carousel music is deafening in my ears. I scream and screech and want to amputate my head from my body.

Pain comes in waves with such force that I have no control I am an animal bellowing, screeching, howling. And then an unstoppable black force bursts inside me. I can do nothing. It controls me.

"Don't push", a voice from inside the carousel chords.

"I can't help it," I cry.

And then three more great bursts and the black thing hurls itself out of me: one, two, three: dragging more shrieks and screams after it, and a great well of water comes with it: a surging flood pond of gush.

"Here he is, here he is," I hear my poet say. He is held in the moment.

I feel a great weight gone: draining in a white crash. I feel so thin as if I would float away. I lift my head and look up

See how tired I look?

"Did he tear me to bits." I say.

I feel ripped and bloody with all that power breaking out of me. I tell her how I lifted my head and saw my son for the first time. He was glistening in a pool of wet, cross and with a stern black frown. He looked so angry at me and life and who could blame him but he *was* nine pounds eleven ounces and I was immensely proud.

Pride and love fills me up as I recount.

And there is Assia in the wave, nodding back at me and rocking Nicholas in his cot while Freida runs around in mirth. And now, inside the wave, I see them from the window of my high up study. I am writing. I am head down in a paper chain. And how I worked : my new gained time alone: a precious gem.

I feel a stirring now inside and music circling my head.

The wave is showing me my new child's upturned face....

'How shall I tell anything at all

To this infant still in a birth-drouse?'

... and I look away but the other Sylvia is on her knees. She is crawling around. She is the animal now: wailing and wailing and wailing at the moon.

The bell is almost as shiny as the panes of glass. I still haven't managed to free the clanger to hear it ring but I work and work on it so I know it will be sometime soon. I am progressing as *we* did, then, our little family. We were so happy at first in our sun-kissed retreat in the countryside of Devon. Our cottage in Court Green grew up with us.

Ted built shelves for books, our prizes and our dreams. I painted and gardened. There were daffodils, strawberry patches hidden in dense screens of holly bushes, wattle fences, fires of wallflowers, and drooping gladioli.

I hung wallpaper patterned by faintly sheened white roses. I baked sponge cakes: six eggs each, from fat hens laying. And then when Assia came, I typed and typed: in piles of sprawled paper over the dull pewter pot of steaming tea.

I wore my brown work pants damp at the knees. My bee hat with netting of nylon sat like a celebration on the brown oak sideboard with stubborn drawers pulled by toddling Freida in her soiled pale blue snowsuit jacket. While Nicholas gurgled the morning songs.

'The womb rattles the pod'

Both my poet and I had accomplished much in the literary world which sometimes seemed like another planet when I was gathering vegetables, and digging potatoes with arms full of tulips and daffodils.

Those tulips should have been *'behind bars like dangerous animals'*.

Of course from time to time I would feel myself slipping away. I always knew when I heard the carousel music. I would begin humming and muttering and flat surfaces would start to curve and the feathered thing inside me would begin to gnaw.

"Are you *alright* Sylvia my poet would say?"

How I hated that he knew. He noticed so when I tried so hard to keep it between me, the tethered bird, and my other self.

....

I don't remember the actual day that my so, so, good neighbour informed me, in words dry and rudderless, that she had 'seen' my poet with another woman. She spooned sugar in her tea in my own kitchen and threw her words to silence me.

Another spoon of sugar. The pitcher of milk, now empty.

"Are you *alright*, Sylvia".

Maybe though she was mistaken she said: perhaps it was only a friend or a sister? Another spoon of sugar from the pot. But didn't his sister live abroad? She was so smug in the comfort of her own vows. Her own husband was so good, so loyal, so faithful, she said.

I beheaded her with a look. No one wants to know from inside hell that someone else's birds are still going tweet, tweet, tweet.

I looked up from my book and felt like throwing it at her. Emily Dickinson could have blackened her eye. Instead, I smiled her off, but even behind my white moon suit and mask veil, her words stung much harder than my bees. I never spoke to that neighbour again. Friends: fiends: demons: black, black witches.

The music circles in my head.

I pulled the phone out of the wall: the phone through which he might have whispered words behind his hand to his whore. I broke it into pieces. I had his head on my wall and I shattered it. The memory of this, releases my demons and I unleash my wrath on the moon

The lioness

The shriek in the bath

The cloak of holes...

And screaming and kicking and hurling rocks, and cursing my stupidity, and my God, and the Angels and the Demons and Life and Death, and Witches and the Devil Moon, I throw myself inside the wave again.

. . . .

My armour is on now and it has to be strong and bullet proof, for I know what's coming next in the wave. I am dried off again and scraping at the bell with such ferocity. My head is a battalion of fixes.

Take hold. Here is the wave.

It throws at me my face contorted with poisoned screams coloured bloody red, devoured and ravished.

"Confess?" I yelled into my poet's thorn eyes.

The dog had peed on the wrong wall. My blind invisible hands were round his neck. They choked each curse out and squeezed his will until it shook the walls.

"Confess?" I bawled.

"You are wringing words out of me," and he plied his poet's voice " I need you to listen, *listen*."

But I was away, rope at the throat, knife twisting in the heart.

I screamed bites and wry words and threw them back and forward then and I moved on to hurling objects. The lamp was thrown, the ornament his mother sent, the gold bound Tibetan Book for the Dead flew like the

Black Demon opening up the swarms of poison to fly around the room.

And then:

We shouted at each other until we raged the storm into a calm of torturous lust.

And then:

The sex was violent. I beat him and he beat me.

And then:

Our feet in the shallows he vowed his allegiance and his forever heart. We were glued together, he said. Nothing could tear us apart. And I felt my scratches tear ridges down his back.

'All true love originates with a wound' he said.

But his tongue was forked.

The hurt inside me burns a hole large in my soul now as then. The wave departs from me: the cursed: and I see my shadow self-drenched by its mire.

And I am thinking that life is temporary so why should death be any different?

There was a Chinese man in a book I was reading at that time inside the wave, of the Tang Dynasty and by which definition, a philosopher. He dreamed he was a butterfly dreaming he was a Chinese philosopher.

I remember envying him so for his twofold security so:

"I decided to dream I was a bee, dreaming I was a poet. What do you think, moon?"

It worked for a while. I convinced myself that my own poet loved only me.

A compromise was reached between the betrayer poet and the betrayed poet and a holiday was agreed upon.

And so two poets inside a wave decide on a change of scene, a vacation to ourselves.

To heal:

To calm.

Ireland was the chosen place away, away, away, we sailed to the green,

green, grass of Eire. Across the sea we sailed.

'The water I taste is warm and salt-

And comes from a country far away as health.

But even in Ireland the grasses always seemed to be running away somewhere into some moon country uninhabited by man.

At first it was calm and beautiful. We stayed in another poet's house. He loved us there we talked of Chaucer, Yeats and Joyce over red, red wine and green, green, vegetables and Irish stews with whiskey in, and Richard Murphy (the poet) let me cook. I was the wife I needed to be, the nurturing one:

But who was nurturing me?

For a while though I forgot or tried to.

And we walked by the sea but words came in on the ebb and flow of the tide: adulterer, adulterer, betrayer, fucker, fucker, fucker.

Richard Murphy took his side of course, men huddled together, bound and stacked like bales of hay. I was being irrational, Richard said

"Are you alright Sylvia?

and *that* did it.

I burned him with my poet at the stake and whoever came to help him: died. I left my 'black marauder' in the night and in the morning let contradictions thrive: let the rain lash and the fire burn down the barn for I was gone. I can't remember then how I got home. Who was minding the children or where I went.

Wave, wave, show me. You know more than me? Show me? I want to kick myself to death. But the wave flows away . I curse, and curse and clatter rocks and …Because I am not at all original:

I throw myself into its depth once more.

....

Does the wave remember the walker upon it?

Is this like in Shakespeare: do all wives come back from the dead?

I am cleaning and scraping the bell again. I have worn myself out cursing and banging my head which bleeds and heals, and bleeds and heals. I have thrown every rock I can hurl against the moon. So, as I say, I am cleaning the bell. Let's get it done.

I am staring at the sky now. Such blackness just as if it were painted in. And now I am taking a rest and lying on the rocks and looking up. Where are the stars that govern life and this miserable death?

"Have I asked you this before moon?"

The whole of life is about the act of letting go and I so want to let go. But I was banished here. While God, if he exists, sends flies to infest wounds that he alone should heal.

I do not look for the wave for I know what happens next.

"Don't look so surprised moon. It is my life you're laundering after all."

So what is next?

Of course my poet tried to sonnet me with his silver tongue.

He pleaded.

He justified.

He twisted and turned.

He tortured.

"Who *is* she?" is all I could say.

The black sky closes in on me. The sea slides back.

"Who is she?" is all I could say.

He would not say her name but continued (despite his declaration and incantations) to deceive, deceive, deceive. And so I burned him at the stake I say and I left him scorched, half man, half fox: singed.

And I howl at the moon again. Is it me or her?

'Mule-bray, pig-grunt and baud cackle

Proceed from your great lips.

It's worse than a barnyard.'

I am the one running while my shadow self stands and watches still.

I roll over and the moon sees me fail.

And then for a long time the wave leaves me alone. It comes and goes with no images contained.

…………………..

I am working the clanger of the bell free.

My mentor, Virginia Woolf, used to work off her depression, not only by sewing patchwork quilts, but by cleaning out her kitchen and cooking haddock and sausages.

Like her, I knew when I was slipping into the black circular pit. The natural necessities created by me: they took over then like an automatic pilot: they took control. I was not happy or unhappy but the 'problem of problems' no longer existed, for they were curved under the carousel tunes which played and played and played repeat.

I scrape and clean and try to smell the fish and meat.

"I nearly have this bell fit to ring out moon. Tell me, that when it rings away the night, that I will be done here?"

The moon stays stubborn and mute and watches as I climb the stairs into the light. Death may whiten in sun or out of it.

I wrote a poem about the moon once. It was rejected by the New Yorker with not so much as a pencil scratch on the black and white doom of the printed rejection. I was so ashamed by it that I hid the letter under a pile of papers like a stillborn illegitimate baby.

I catch my image in the pane I am cleaning and it tells me the moon will never find out all the things I hide. Nor will he understand how the tethered bird lies in wait, deep down inside me and moves his feathers when the carousel turns.

The moon is not that clever. I tell him what I want him to hear: nothing.

CHAPTER 11

WAVE 1962

• REVELATIONS

I have cleaned the rope again which holds the bell.

I have worked it free. My shadow self is back and screaming

"Free! free! free?"

The moon seems on her side. But would I and will do what I did all over again to spite them both? The rope is strong and dry in this world preoccupied with water. I am forming the rope into a noose.

The moon is blanketed in bees. Z z z z z...

The beam which holds the rope is also strong. It swings above the flight of stairs. And I remember, again a rope which once I formed to pretend I would strangle my mother. I practiced on the air.

"Mother, mother, I will choke the life out of you!"

I throw the moon a glance.

His cratered dome is down as I pile up the stones:

one,

two,

three,

four.

One more slab of stone and I can reach the hanging noose. I will confuse you moon with déjà vu.

My shadow self has called out to the moon. The moon wakes suddenly, sour, sweet honeyed onion now. He makes a move and sends the signal to the wave. I lull him into thinking what I *make* him think.

And I add to this, by quoting Joyce at him.

'Hold onto the now, the here, through which all future plunges to the past.'

He is clouded now for he is confused trying to work out where he heard these words before (just as Joyce himself intended so.)

....

I have swung, head in the noose till my breath stinks of the terrors that had killed me many times before.

Will you ever understand? The other Sylvia has stopped running.

My eyes are wet. There are new tears in my nightshirt now: tears and tears.

But I am back again from death, sitting on the highest rock and hugging my knees. I am the bottom of an upturned glass. The moon is its circular rim. The water behind my eyes shows me the darkest time of all where my path narrowed into a tiny curved relentless line. '*And the snares almost effaced themselves.* '

I had taken the children up to London to see my friend, Assia.

I needed to tell someone. The hurt of adultery needed to be spoken out loud.

'*How we need another soul to cling to.*'

And the process of telling might make me see some solution from:- '*The constriction killing me also.*' I timed it so that David, Assia's husband would be at work for he had never liked me and would be sure to take Ted's side against mine.

But when I arrived at Primrose Hill, it was David who answered the door. Assia was out, he said. He did not seem to know where she was, or when she'd be back, and he was curt. He showed me into the kitchen to wait then closed the door on my children and me and went upstairs.

Left in the kitchen that had once been mine, I settled the children and looked about me. I could sense part of me still there. I walked around disentangling limbs, and loves, and lives. A groundswell of memory fluttered under my gaze.

While my children twitched and fretted both in the one pram, the rainy curtains of a cold September snipped at their stems. I hushed and tucked and wondered if Freida recognised her former home: a tiny wisp of the familiar perhaps, but I dared not let her free to roam.

The kitchen had lost our stamp. Its walls were painted over pale: a clock ticked away in metal curves: a paraffin heater gurgled its lucent blue petrol and a wire red dome tried to warm the room.

David came back in and hovered around.

"Do you think this is wise," he said.

I was taken aback. I waited for some explanation and the front door opened, cutting through his words.

And Assia came. Her hair was wild with the wind, her shoulders wet with rain. She said something curtly to David then turned and saw me. Standing up to greet her, I felt her back away.

"*Sylvia*" she said and made my name feel like a question. Her mouth stayed open but no more words came:

'Zeros shutting on nothing.'

Had David turned her against me? Surely she would not take Ted's side against mine?

"Sylvia," she said again. I'm sorry...I...*we*... never planned...I didn't mean...

Her face melted a weeping glitter. Her eyes fell on some point way above my head. Her red nailed hands rubbed together.

Her head was hung.

"I'm sorry." she said behind a veil.

And then and only then: truth screeched towards me from a pinpoint of light in the corner of her blinking eye. And suddenly I realised.

And I stood tied and gagged. I could not undo myself.

And then this flickering Judas dared to stand in front of me and utter words.

"I am… Ted and I... we are *so* sorry".

"*We*", she dared to say and twisted and turned the arrow in the wound.

Then hell hurled flames inside my mind: with the smoke of the fire that I had lit unwittingly. They tore around inside my mouth before they flew out in raged curses, coloured red and orange, and black and black and black…

My roar was like a basement furnace.

"It was *you, you, **you**.*"

The music from the fiery carousel was loud and crass: the bird face with slashed red lips it laughed and laughed and screamed in fire till I was bled dry, burned and spinning round on some toy of noise and lights that flashed and flashed and would not halt.

"Are you alright, Sylvia."

I felt so still and empty then. The way the eye of a tornado must feel, I thought. I felt as if I were standing still and silent, centred in the middle of a mind full of lashing chaos.

And deep inside the wave I watched me fall apart. The pieces of me floated away and came back lodged in wrong sequence.

My life was spewed out at my feet for the very thing I had most feared had happened. I had dwelt on it too long. It had the courage denied to me. Was it a punishment then, or a reward?

....

My children kept me sewn together after that, with just some stitches dropped along the way.

The countryside of my devoted Devon was left behind, my vegetables to rot, my flowers to wither, my bees to hum themselves to death. They were all undertakers then.

For he had flown off with the new bee; Sting.

But no, wait, moon, I am doing bees some ill. A bee is far too good for her she was more akin to a spider demon. Yes, she was a Joro-Gumo who sought out men like you moon, to poison, crucify, then eat."

The moon falters and shines all around him like some spent torch.

....

Now I have worn myself out cursing and throwing rocks at the sky, the wave, and at the moon. It is the way I exercise and now I am lying face down on the rocks so I cannot see the moon's ugly face. The slime is in my mouth.

How long I have lain I do not know but I am hoping to eat the ground and let the water wash over me till I change: the sea change, Ariel? I will mould into part crust and slime and a film of salt will form over me and I will become something else.

I am not fussy just anything other than who or what I am.

I taste the salt night on my tongue: a serpent. The slime is me. My eyes see colours in the surface of the rock behind my closed lids. My ears hear the wave wail and the bat calls echoes inside my mind for I am lost.

I am smothered. My anger has left me polarised.

I am trapped in Prosperous pine and ranting and raging to be free. I have been lying face down for so long the will is nearly burned away and I am nearly flayed raw.

I have imagined that Juro Gumo with her tentacles entwined choking out my poet's screams of ecstasy.

I have dwelt on her lips spewed with his sticky, smelling, semen. I have seen her swallow black, sweet, blood mouthfuls of mine, mine, mine. I have listened to him lavish fucked up words composed of underworldly passion for her green insides.

And even now when the wave has gone, my mind is filled with the tortured intensity of self: my biggest cut of all. I yearned for it. I handed him to her on a velvet plate. She ate him plate and balls and all. It makes me sick. I am a black Red Riding Hood watching my wolf life play out for all to see: Eat me, chew me, spit me out.

I feel my shadow self. I feel her hurt for me. I feel her warmth. But still she will not open her eyes to me.

CHAPTER 12

• LAST CHAPTER

WAVE DECEMBER 1962

'Oh, only left to myself, what a poet I will flay myself into'.

"So moon, you have seen me cut up and humiliated, seen me sullied and ruined, now I will show my readers how I rose again?"

"I will show them how it is, that when you perfect your own mind, you become your very own Lighthouse."

'Does not my heat astound you. And my light.'

The secret key with the sacred number, turns to lock or unlock?

The pane of glass is frosted inside the wave. It is frosted from the inside out. It's winter. It must be 1962 for I have moved my cut up mind and my children to 23 Fitzroy Square in Primrose Hill. I see the other number on the door.

I am alone: a single mother of two. Maturity of sorts, begins.

Inside the wave I am planning. Each week I must make up some new outpost to conquer, first I will try to sleep without pills, will write a letter, and cut the children's hair to tidy them up. Victories however small. I must shoulder my aloneness somehow and begin to be nobler. I must be well.

I must appreciate. I put down my pen and look around. I have found a pretty place to nest my children. I see it now. W. B. Yeats once lived in the house. I am deep in philosophical thought inside the wave. I resolve to heal into this poet house and this time I must let the world come back to me. Look how white and clean the house is. And outside the window matches. It is pure and starched and coated in snow.

And I am writing again these words :

'I...Have a self to recover, a queen.

Is she dead, is she sleeping?

Where has she been ,

With her lion-red body, her wings of glass?'

The wave is showing me an image of me now back at my desk. I am writing and writing and writing till my wrist hurts with pain.

My novel is nearly finished now.

'

Now she is flying

More terrible than ever was, red

Scar in the sky. '

See, reader:

Without him I live.

Without him I work.

Without him I achieve.

Ariel, angel of the waters of the earth, have you been watching this: have you been taking it in?

The wave vomits my image away and washes my achievement inside its veins and sinews and coughs it back without a thought.

Myself unfolds like a suit, with pockets of fulfilled dreams.

The once desired image of me as the domestic goddess: wife, mother, homemaker, protector of the wholesome, the good and the holy had so let me down and kicked a hole inside my head which I have now filled with the new me.

And now, there is a wild green in the air, and the blood jet is poetry.

I see myself within the wave and I am utterly true to myself, utterly detached, completely an artist. I have turned on the other scenario. That, 'oh so good' domestic goddess: the past was all her doing, my shadow self. She had trapped me so with all of this:

-*'Measuring the flour, cutting off the surplus, Adhering to rules, to rules, to rules'.*

My God, what a laugh! This is one for the annunciation!

Listen readers and take note: It is fitting that this book of mine is coming to its end. There will be forty-nine pauses. The key is turned. Ted had been to the house to collect the last of his things. Even that did not slow my writing pace. I worked through it all, through the day and through the night.

He did not matter. He did not even exist: only my art was real. I described myself.

'I am a lantern.

My Head is a moon

Of Japanese paper, my gold beaten skin infinitely delicate and infinitely expensive.'

Now I was free, free of that gag in my throat and free of him.

'A pure acetylene Virgin

Attended by roses,

By kisses, by cherubim, . .

-(My selves dissolving, old whore petticoats)

To Paradise. '

A bee, I worked myself to death!

I took my rightful place inside the poetic world flanked by Otto and the Mother/Other. I was me. I was the magician girl who did not flinch.

Ariel was my ethereal spirit hauling me through the air letting go all hostilities: keeping myself, it seems, in a state of miraculous repair .

I accumulated over forty poems.

I *do* see now though, how dangerously altered and alienated my state of mind was then. I had lost interest for the highest stake in the game of living, life itself, had not been risked. But it took the ruin of my other, my shadow self, to write with this kind of artistry?

It had been a fight to the death. One of us had to die.

I write that death was my lover then?

'This death, this death?-

Is this the one sin then,

This old dead love of death?'

But if this is just a verse of mind, the other is true fact. The poems I wrote then were my Ariel poems.

The best poems that I had ever written.

'The woman is perfected.

Her dead

Body wears the smile of accomplishment -'

I am contrite and exorcised in this dead space. It is *I* now, and not the moon, in control of it all and all exists. And I have the rope fixed now to hang the bell and I am searching for some more flat stones so that I can reach to attach the two ends of the rope together to hear the bell ring out.

Two ends of the same rope.

Now I see my shadow self. She is walking towards me. Her spindly arms are swinging up and down. Does she not feel her fate? I turn quickly to face her and fall and tumble on the stair. I am on my knees. I sit down and inspect and the moon shines low between my legs and lights me up.

My shadow self is climbing up towards me now.

'-No kin of mine,

yet kin she is

Riddled with ghosts to lie deadlocked with them

Taking roots as cradles rock...'

She is facing me. Her eyes are down. But slowly now she raises up her eyes to mine and stretches out her hand.

The caged bird leaps. And at her touch I feel what she feels. My heart is cut. Stenches and colours assail me. The stigma of selfhood bleeds through my lines. I am a pulse that wanes and wanes.

And I am on my knees to all the hurt, to all the wounds, and to the twisted guts and innards of the tethered bird which scrapes and scrapes in flickering light. She, my shadow self, lifts me up and out and disentangles all my turning knots and flattens all the curves and all the grooves of old faults deep and bitter.

And I see straight through the black. It's dark. It's black and gold and crimson too.

'-Berries cast dark Hooks

Black sweet blood mouthfuls

Shadows'-

The water folds around me. Her arms fold around me, Ariel's cloak.

There is light.

There *is* coherence. Since that moment in time: it is enclosed in eternity.

And hear?

The bell is ringing out. It rings and rings and rings and rings. It reaches down-

'Something hauls me through the air

Thighs,

hair, flakes from my heels'

And I am held
Tight:
'My
I,my
selves
dissolving'-as
It pulls me up
        up
         up
        up
         up
        up
inside my light.

The window of the children's room is wide open now. And, in flux of light and time, alive with blue-grey moths, and they are flying and flying and flying...

...and flying.

THE END

ABOUT THE AUTHOR

Dr Joyce Garvey is a working artist and writer. Her previous books are : 'The Girl with the Monkey on her Shoulder' published by Original Writing Ltd 2016, 'Lucia, The Girl who Danced in Shadows' published in 2018 and 'Sylvia, 'The Girl who Talked to the Moon' to be published 2019.

'Edinburgh, Festival of Murder', crime novel. Published 2019.

52858075R00083

Made in the USA
Lexington, KY
23 September 2019